Paw Prints

ISBN: 978-1-7338906-0-1 (Hardcover)
ISBN: 9781095556757 (Paperback)

Story and Book design by Morgan J Muir
www.morganjmuir.com

Illustrations by Sava "SuperGalaxyFox" Andreea

For my Skye Watcher
Who was everything to us a dog should be.
We miss you.

They say that pets will leave paw prints on my heart.
But I don't think that I believe them.

There are paw prints in the snow and on my floor
and on the rug.

But they'll disappear before the dawn.

There are paw prints in the concrete,
But my heart's not made of stone.

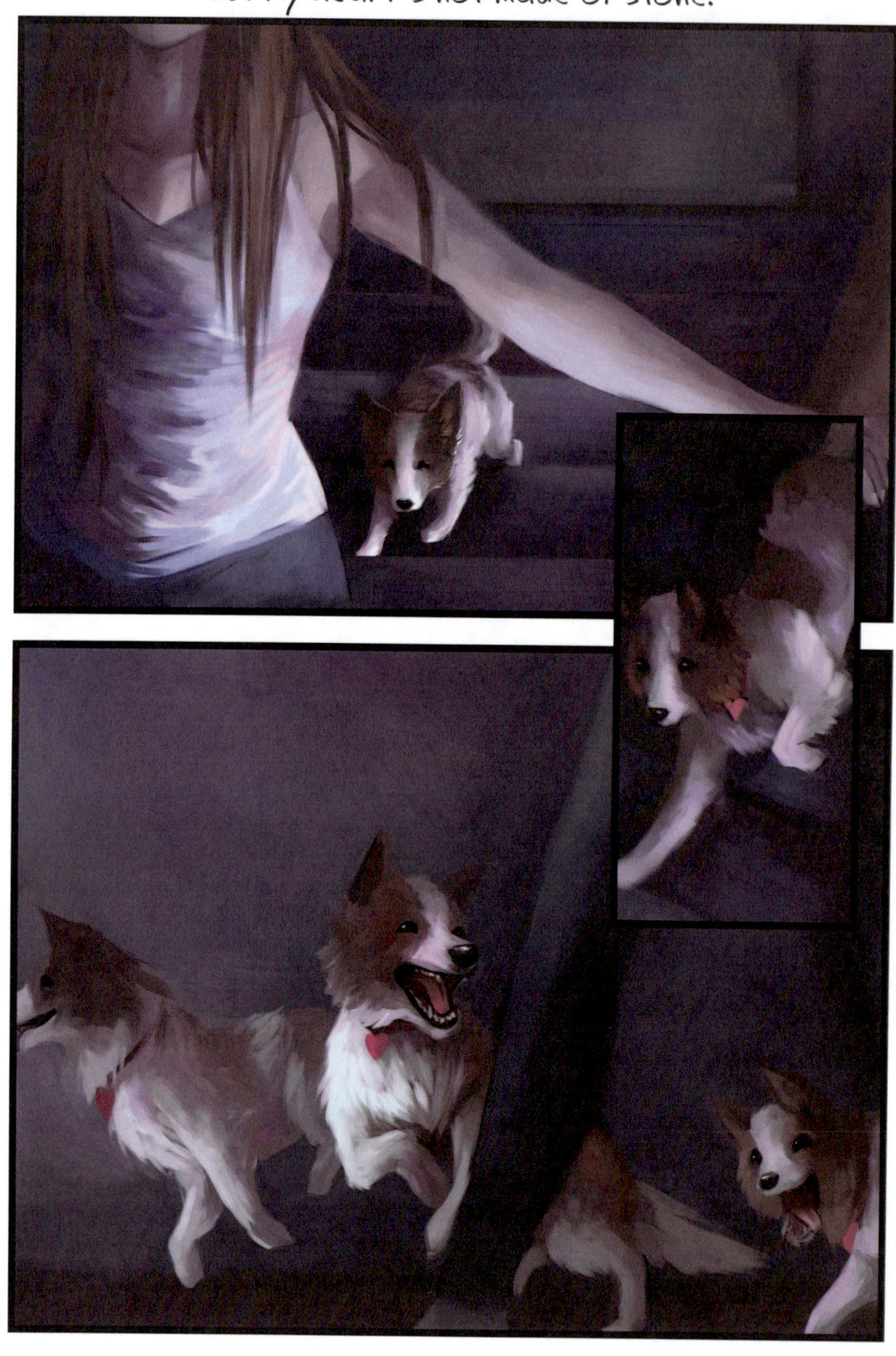

There is fur in the couch and in your bed and on my clothes.
A wash, a clean, a vacuum and that, too, will soon be gone.

I could, perhaps, douse my heart in soap and tears,
But I'm not sure even that would soak away your loss.

There are teeth marks on the toys and couch and chairs.
Marks that will not fade with time.

From your youthful, nipping play.

It's not paw prints on my heart I feel

Paw prints never hurt this way.

Afterword

From the time I was very young I have loved to tell stories, usually of magic and talking animals. I very distinctly remember the day I realized that I could write the stories down instead of just telling them to myself. That day something truly magical was born. Ever since, I have felt a pressing need to share the stories rattling around in my head.

Paw Prints is a bit of a deviation from my normal brand of storytelling. Along with a love of stories, I have always loved animals. I grew up with horses, cats, and dogs, but it wasn't until recently that I got to pick for myself my first pet (my current cats were rescued as five day old kittens who'd been abandoned; they chose me). It is amazing how quickly a puppy can worm its way into your heart, and when I lost her I was heartbroken. This story was born from that heartbreak, filling my head and demanding to be shared. Thank you for sharing it with me.

Morgan J Muir

* 9 7 8 1 7 3 3 8 9 0 6 0 1 *